For Biddle's Sake

For Biddle's Sake

Gail Carson Levine
ILLUSTRATED BY Mark Elliott

■ HarperCollins*Publishers*

For Biddle's Sake

Text copyright © 2002 by Gail Carson Levine

Illustrations copyright © 2002 by Mark Elliott

Printed in the United States of America. All rights reserved.

www.harperchildrens.com

Library of Congress Cataloging-in-Publication Data

Levine, Gail Carson.

For Biddle's sake / Gail Carson Levine ; illustrated by Mark Elliott.

p.   cm.

"The princess tales."

Summary: In this humorous retelling of Andrew Lang's "Puddocky,"
a young maiden who has been transformed into a toad by a jealous
fairy relies on her newly honed magical abilities to charm a prince
into marriage.

ISBN 0-06-000094-5 — ISBN 0-06-000095-3 (lib. bdg.)

[1. Fairy tales.   2. Magic—Fiction.   3. Princes—Fiction.]

I. Elliott, Mark, ill.

PZ8.L4793Fo   2002   2001039287

[Fic]—dc21   CIP

                                                              AC

Typography by Michele Tupper

3   4   5   6   7   8   9   10

❖

First Edition

All my love to Rani and Ronnie—
friend, fellow artist, sister.

—G.C.L.

BOOKS BY
Gail Carson Levine

Ella Enchanted
Dave at Night
The Wish
The Two Princesses of Bamarre

THE PRINCESS TALES:

The Fairy's Mistake
The Princess Test
Princess Sonora and the Long Sleep
Cinderellis and the Glass Hill
The Fairy's Return

Betsy Who Cried Wolf

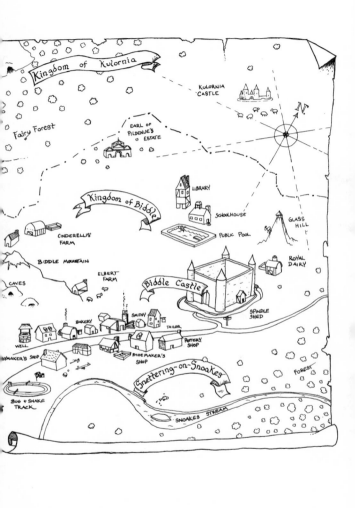

One

When she was two years old, Patsy tasted a sprig of parsley at a traveling fair. She loved it, and from that moment on, the only food she would eat was parsley. After a while her parents, Nelly and Zeke, began to call her that, Parsley.

The trouble was that parsley grew in only one spot in the village of Snettering-on-Snoakes, and that spot was the garden of the fairy Bombina, who was renowned for turning people into toads.

Nelly said she couldn't let her daughter

starve, and Zeke, who rarely spoke, nodded.

So every Thursday night, Zeke would head for Rosella Lane, where he'd climb the high wall that surrounded the fairy's garden. He'd stuff a sack full of fresh parsley and return home. His stealing went undetected for three years because Bombina was serving time in the dungeon of Anura, the fairy queen. Bombina's crime was failure to get along with humans.

Meanwhile, Parsley grew into a plump, happy child with a lovely smile, in spite of teeth that were stained a pale green.

Then Bombina returned.

That Thursday evening, she strolled in her garden and saw Zeke gathering armloads of parsley. Armloads! She would have turned him into a toad on the spot, but she had already reached Anura's legal limit of five human-to-toad transformations per fairy per year, and she didn't want to go back to jail.

"What are you doing?" she shrieked.

Zeke grabbed the parsley and ran. Bombina stood on her left foot and blinked twice. Zeke froze, unable to move a muscle. Bombina thought of turning him to stone, but stone wasn't her specialty. Her specialty was toads.

"Why are you stealing my parsley?" she thundered. Then she unfroze Zeke's mouth.

Zeke wasn't used to talking. So even though his mouth could move, it didn't.

Bombina dropped her voice to a sugary whisper. "I can turn you into a chicken . . ." She never ran out of legal chicken transformations. "A clucking—"

3

Zeke found his voice. "It's for m-my d-daughter."

His daughter? Anura always said that fairies should be kind to children. Fairies who were kind were her favorites. Bombina was on probation, and she was definitely not one of the fairy queen's favorites.

"Bring your daughter to me."

"B-but—"

"Bring your daughter to me!" Bombina unfroze all of Zeke.

He stumbled once, then started to run.

"And drop the parsley."

Back in their cottage Zeke told Nelly what Bombina had commanded. Nelly began to run around frantically, bumping into Zeke and shouting that she wasn't bringing her precious daughter to anybody. Zeke ran around frantically too, and he bumped into Nelly when she wasn't bumping into him.

4

Bombina materialized in the cottage, right next to Parsley's bed. "Is this your daughter?"

Parsley awoke and sat up, blinking in the bright light that flashed around Bombina's big pink wings.

"Hello, child," Bombina boomed.

Parsley was frightened. She'd never seen anyone so enormous or so grumpy-looking.

"What's your name, honey?"

Parsley said, "Parsley," in a small voice.

"*Parsley!*" Bombina whirled on Nelly and Zeke. "You dared to name your daughter after my parsley?"

Nelly held her ground. "We named her P-Patsy, Your G-Graciousness, but—"

"Silence!" Bombina leaned over the bed. "Why do you like parsley so much, Parsley?"

Parsley didn't know why. She just did.

She stared at Bombina and didn't say anything.

"Answer the nice fairy," Nelly said. "Tell her why . . ."

She's a fairy? Parsley thought. She'd been taught that fairies were gentle and good. Then this one was only pretending to be mean. She smiled up at Bombina.

Nothing was sweeter than Parsley's smile.

A tiny corner of Bombina's heart melted. "Harrumph." She cleared her throat. And had a brilliant idea. Anura would be delighted! "I will take the child home to live with me. Then Parsley can eat parsley whenever she likes."

Live with a fairy! Parsley was thrilled. Maybe she'd learn magic. "Can I, Mama?"

A tear trickled down Nelly's cheek.

A tear trickled down Zeke's cheek.

"Well?" Bombina yelled. "Can she?"

Nelly and Zeke couldn't refuse a fairy. Nelly said, "Yes, Parsley gumdrop, you can go."

Two

Nearby in Biddle Castle, Prince Tansy was in the throne room with his brothers, Prince Randolph and Prince Rudolph, who were arguing as usual. Randolph and Rudolph were twins, and they were nine years old, two years older than Tansy. No one else was in the room.

Tansy could tell the twins apart because Randolph's left nostril was slightly larger than his right nostril, and Rudolph's right nostril was slightly larger than his left.

"The right hand, fool!" Randolph held King Humphrey IV's gilded wooden scepter just beyond Rudolph's reach. "A king holds the scepter in his right hand."

"The left hand, numskull!" Rudolph twisted Randolph's nose and tried to grab the scepter.

With his free hand Randolph twisted Rudolph's nose.

Tansy removed Rudolph's fingers from Randolph's nose and Randolph's fingers from Rudolph's nose. He said, "I think—"

"You don't have to think," Randolph said, trying to grab some part of Rudolph again.

"You'll never be king, Tansy," Rudolph said, lunging for the scepter and getting one hand on it.

Randolph tried to yank the scepter away from Rudolph.

Rudolph hung on and tried to yank it away from Randolph.

Tansy said, "Stop! You'll break it."

Crack! The scepter broke in half.

Randolph and Rudolph dropped their halves and ran out of the throne room. Tansy ran too, although he knew what was going to happen next. The Royal Guards were going to find the three of them. Randolph and Rudolph were going to tell King Humphrey IV that he, Tansy, had broken the scepter, and King Humphrey IV was going to believe them, no matter what Tansy said. Then the king was going to make him write *I will never again break a Royal Scepter* at least a hundred times.

While Tansy ran, he thought about the question his brothers had been arguing over. The solution was simple. A king should hold his scepter in his right hand on Sundays, Tuesdays, and Fridays, and in the left on Mondays, Thursdays, and Saturdays. That would show how fair he was. He should hold it with both hands on Wednesdays. That would show how stable his kingdom was.

Randolph and Rudolph hadn't thought the matter through. They never did.

But one of them would be king anyway, and Tansy never would be, even though he had hundreds of great ideas about how to rule the kingdom of Biddle. Youngest sons didn't become king.

Bombina liked having Parsley live with her. She especially liked having Parsley's smile live with her. She'd do anything to see that smile, and anything included some surprising things—smiling back at Parsley or occasionally smiling first, tucking Parsley in at night, and even letting Parsley touch her wings. Bombina had never let anyone do that before.

For her part, Parsley loved living in the fairy's palace, although she missed Nelly and Zeke. Bombina's cook knew dozens of parsley recipes. Parsley could have her parsley scrambled, steamed, stewed, barbecued, braised, broiled, fried, or liquefied. She could have parsley pesto, parsley pasta, parsley pizza, parsley pilaf, or parsley in puff pastry. And for dessert she could have parsley pie, parsley pudding, parsley penuche, parsley taffy, parsley upside-down cake, or, the one she liked best, parsley ice cream sundae with hot parsley sauce and parsley sprinkles on top.

But most of all Parsley loved watching Bombina make magic.

The fairy never used a wand. She began all her magic by standing on her left foot. To disappear, she'd make her chin jut forward and put her left pinky finger in her mouth. And *poof!* she'd be gone. To sink into the ground, she'd bend at the waist and hop twice. A hole would appear, and she'd slide into it till only her head showed.

But the magic that Bombina did most often was to turn objects into toads. The fairy queen's limit applied only to humans—Bombina could transform as many of anything else as she liked.

Parsley was astonished at the things Bombina turned into toads—a single thread in a bodice, an egg, a tile roof, a picture frame, an umbrella handle.

Once, when her footman Stanley failed to open the carriage door quickly enough, Bombina turned his bushy red beard into a purple Fury-Faced Trudy Toad. It looked funny, hanging upside down from Stanley's chin. Bombina

"BOMBINA TURNED HIS BUSHY RED BEARD

INTO A PURPLE FURY-FACED TRUDY TOAD."

laughed, and Parsley would have too if Stanley hadn't looked utterly shocked.

Parsley tried to cast spells too. For example, she'd let her hot parsley tea cool. Then she'd stand on her left foot, lick her index fingers, and grunt *ung huh tuh* exactly as Bombina would. But her tea never warmed up. She couldn't fly either, or make her slippers come to her from halfway across the bedchamber.

She never tried to turn anything into a toad. It didn't seem right. Maybe Stanley's beard was pleased to be a toad, but maybe it wasn't. Maybe it didn't like croaking and catching flies.

Once Parsley asked Bombina, "Why can't I make magic? It looks simple when you do it." She smiled.

As usual, Bombina was enchanted by the smile. That's another kind of magic, she thought, to be able to smile so charmingly with teeth as green as a green onion.

"You have to be magical to make magic, dear. I'm a magical creature, and you aren't."

Three

Parsley had been living with Bombina for ten months when June 23, Midsummer's Eve, the fairies' New Year, came around. As always, Bombina attended the ball at Anura's palace, where she received, along with the other fairies, her new allotment of legal transformations.

During the ball Bombina told the fairy queen about adopting Parsley. Anura clapped her hands in joy. "Hurrah, Bombina! With your little Oregano you will—"

"Parsley," Bombina said.

"Ah, yes. You will usher in a golden age in your Snetting-Snooks. You and your Tarragon will—"

"Snettering-on-Snoakes. Parsley."

"Whatever. A river of love will flow from humans to you and from you to them. You won't want to turn a single one, not even the most aggravating, into a toad." Anura embraced Bombina and bathed her face in kisses.

When Parsley went into Bombina's bedroom the next morning, Bombina sat up instantly. She couldn't wait to begin her new life of deep and abiding friendship with humans.

"Come here, child." And she kissed Parsley on the forehead.

Parsley didn't know about the fairies' New Year or what Anura had said, but she liked the kiss. She smiled and said, "How are you going to wear your hair today?" She thought Bombina's hairstyling magic was the best magic of all.

"We'll see." Bombina knew Parsley liked to watch, so she decided to try out a few new styles until the serving maid brought breakfast. She sat at her dressing table. Parsley came and stood next to her.

Bombina shook out her long red hair. Then she lifted her right foot, stuck out her front teeth, and said *arr arr arr*. Her hair shrank into her scalp until only a couple of inches were left, and those inches curled into ringlets. She knocked her fists together, and her hair turned blue with blond stripes.

Parsley giggled.

Bombina's stomach rumbled. She frowned. Where was that lazy serving maid?

Ah, well, Bombina thought. Perhaps Cook was preparing something special to please her. Bombina stuck out her chin and said *raa raa raa*. Her hair grew long again and piled itself on top of her head.

"Oooh!" Parsley said.

Bombina's stomach rumbled again. She didn't want something special. She wanted her ordinary breakfast at its ordinary time. But it was too late for that. *I must calm myself,* she thought. *Perhaps the serving maid was carrying my breakfast to me when she fell and broke both her ankles. That would be nice.*

Bombina stood up and started to pace.

Uh-oh! Parsley thought. She got out of the way and stood in the window alcove.

Bombina paced and thought. *Perhaps Cook fell into the porridge and drowned. That would be nice too.*

In fact, the serving maid had quit the night before. The servants knew that the fairies' New Year always brought new toad transformations. Bombina had been kinder lately, but they were still frightened. The year before Bombina had gone to jail, she had turned three gardeners, a manservant, and a seamstress into toads.

No one wanted to deliver Bombina's breakfast. After arguing for a half hour, the servants ganged up on the scullery wench, who had started her job only the week before. Cook carried the breakfast tray to Bombina's door, and two menservants carried the wench. When they got there, Cook put the tray into the scullery wench's hands. One manservant opened the door, and the other shoved her inside.

"There you are!" Bombina shouted while shifting her weight onto her left foot. Then she began to stare at the scullery wench. She lowered her chin to her chest and continued to stare.

Oh, no! Parsley thought. She's going to—

Bombina flapped her right wing once while singing *oople toople* in a high scratchy voice.

The scullery wench looked startled. Parsley heard the beginning of a yelp. The breakfast tray clattered to the floor, and the scullery wench shrank. For a moment she stood there, an orange scullery wench two inches tall. Then she was a toad, an orange Christopher Inquisitive Toad.

Parsley wanted to scream, but she couldn't, or she might be turned into a toad too. She slipped behind the window drapes and peeked through them.

Bombina hiccuped twice, and the toad vanished. She noticed the smashed breakfast tray on the tile floor. Her yummy coddled eggs were a yellow puddle, and her lovely porridge with figs and raisins was hardening into a big brown lump.

She was so angry, she stamped her feet and shrieked *aargh* and accidentally turned a candlestick into a feathered bonnet. Then she stormed out of her bedchamber.

A minute later Parsley crept out too, gladder than ever before to still have two human legs and two human hands and no warts.

Within a quarter hour Cook was a mauve Sir Melvin Dancing Toad, the two menservants were both turquoise Belladonna Spinning Toads, and the laundress, who happened to be in the kitchen, was an ultramarine Ethelinda Bumbling Toad. Bombina had beaten her own record for using up toad transformations.

Four

Parsley felt terrible about the toads. She had liked all of them when they were human, and she had especially liked Cook. Parsley was almost certain that toads ate their food raw, and Cook would hate that.

Bombina did everything she could think of to cheer Parsley up and get her smiling again. The fairy found a new cook who knew a hundred parsley recipes, including one for parsley bubble gum.

Parsley blew big green bubbles, but she wouldn't smile.

Bombina invented fifteen new hairdos, but Parsley still wouldn't smile.

Bombina gave Parsley a magic spyglass that could see anything anywhere in Biddle, no matter what was in the way.

But Parsley still wouldn't smile.

Bombina was frantic. She begged Parsley to smile. She shouted. She wept.

But Parsley still wouldn't smile.

Finally, in desperation, Bombina said, "I won't turn people into toads anymore."

Parsley smiled.

Bombina was so happy that she hugged Parsley with both arms and both wings. But while she hugged, she thought, By next New Year, Parsley will have forgotten my promise.

Parsley loved her magic spyglass. She looked through it at Zeke and Nelly and the new baby. She looked over all of

Biddle. She saw Elroy the shepherd's great-great-grandson herd sheep. She saw Ralph's and Burt's grandchildren do their farm chores, and once she even saw Ralph and Burt themselves, sitting on their porch, rocking back and forth, perfectly in time with each other.

Parsley watched the Royal Banquets in Biddle Castle, examining the plates for parsley dishes. She watched the Royal Balls, searching for ladies' hairdos that Bombina could try out. Once she saw a hair ornament atop an especially tall hairdo—a miniature sailing ship, with all sails billowing.

The first time Parsley saw the Royal Family was at a banquet. King Humphrey IV was bald, and his ears stuck out. The twins, Prince Randolph and Prince Rudolph, would have been handsome if they had ever stopped glaring at each other. The youngest prince, Prince Tansy, had freckles, a cowlick, and a serious expression. Parsley thought he looked exactly the way a prince should.

One twin sat on the king's right and the other sat on his left, and they glared at each other around King Humphrey IV's belly. Tansy sat farther down the banquet table, between two Royal Councillors.

The twin on King Humphrey IV's left cut his baked potato the long way, but the twin on the right cut his potato the short way. The twin on the left ate in this order: roast hart, potato, lentils, watercress. The twin on the right ate in the reverse order.

All Tansy was eating was the watercress. Parsley was thrilled. He loved watercress and she loved parsley. They had something in common!

Actually, they didn't. Tansy never ate more than one dish at any meal, so he could give it his undivided attention. The watercress was pretty good, but he didn't love it.

The next time Parsley observed Tansy, he was in the Royal Wardrobe Room with his two brothers. The twins were both trying on King Humphrey IV's red satin Royal Ceremonial Robe. One twin had his arm in the left sleeve and the other had his arm in the right sleeve. Each was struggling to pull the robe away from the other.

They were caroming from one side of the room to the other—smashing into the shelves that held the king's breeches, corsets, codpieces, garters, jerkins, and undershirts. Tansy was dodging the flying Royal Wardrobe and saying something.

Oh no! The Royal Ceremonial Robe was ripping, up from the filigreed hem all the way to the ermine collar.

Now the twins were pulling off the robe and running out of the Royal Wardrobe Room, with Tansy right behind them. Parsley followed him in her spyglass. He dashed through the castle, out a first-floor window, along a cobblestone path, and into the Royal Museum of Quest Souvenirs, where he threw himself into the pile of straw under the turkey that lays tin eggs.

He wormed his way in so far that only the tippy toe of one boot stuck out, and Parsley feared he wouldn't get enough air to breathe.

She turned her spyglass back to the castle, where a search was in progress. A Royal Guard found one twin hiding

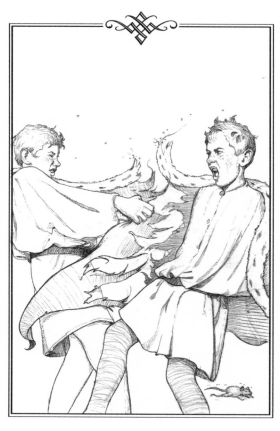

"OH NO! THE ROYAL CEREMONIAL ROBE

WAS RIPPING."

under a bed in a Royal Bedchamber. Another guard found the other twin under a bed in a different Royal Bedchamber.

Randolph and Rudolph don't have much imagination, Parsley thought, feeling proud of Tansy for hiding in such a good spot. She watched the Royal Guards search Biddle Castle from the cellar to the towers. Then she joined Bombina for lunch.

After lunch Parsley watched the Royal Guards search the Royal Stable, the Royal Dairy, and Queen Sonora's old spindle shed. They searched the museum last and finally found Tansy, who emerged covered with straw and bits of tin. He looked sad and scared. Parsley's heart went out to him.

The Royal Guards marched him to the throne room, where his brothers and

King Humphrey IV were waiting. Randolph and Rudolph pointed at Tansy. Parsley saw their mouths shape the words *Tansy did it. He ripped the Royal Robe.*

But he didn't! Parsley thought. He didn't do anything.

King Humphrey IV yanked Tansy up by his ear and shook him. Then he dragged Tansy out of the throne room. Randolph and Rudolph watched him go. They were both grinning.

Royal Rats! Parsley thought.

With the spyglass she followed Tansy and King Humphrey IV along the Royal First Floor Corridor, up the Royal West Tower Stairway, up, up, up to a room at the top of the tower, where there were a desk and a chair and ink and parchment and a quill pen and nothing else. King Humphrey IV left Tansy there, and the prince sat at the desk and began to write.

Parsley focused her spyglass on the parchment and saw—

I will never again rip the Royal Robe.
I will never again rip the Royal Robe.
I will never again rip the Royal Robe.
I will never again rip the Royal Robe.
I will never again rip the Royal Robe.

A tear fell on the parchment and blurred three lines of *never again*. Parsley felt like crying too.

Five

By the time Parsley was fifteen, she had watched Randolph and Rudolph get Tansy in trouble for scores of things he hadn't done—denting the Royal Armor, laming the Royal Steed, breaking the hand off the marble statue of King Humphrey I, and releasing the flea big enough to fill a teacup from the Royal Museum of Quest Souvenirs.

The flea was the worst. It bit King Humphrey IV, and his cheek swelled as big as a teakettle. Tansy spent a whole week in the Royal West Tower that time.

Parsley despised Randolph and

Rudolph. She half wanted Tansy to punch each of them in their Royal Noses, but she admired him no end for his forbearance. Whenever she saw him in the spyglass, she smiled and smiled.

One day, Bombina saw her smiling and was instantly jealous. "What's so special out there?" she roared.

"Nothing," Parsley said nervously. "Just the roses in Biddle Castle's garden." Bombina hadn't turned anyone into a toad since she'd promised not to nine years ago, but Parsley knew she still could. She smiled at the fairy. "Our roses are better, though."

Bombina relaxed. She marveled, as she often did, that she had given up her hobby—her art—for this lass. Bombina had felt dreadfully deprived at first, but then she'd discovered that *not* turning people into toads gave her a delightful sense of power. Since she never used up her yearly limit, she could always turn someone into a toad if she wanted to. And she still turned objects into toads, so her skills hadn't gotten rusty.

⚓ ⚓ ⚓

The next day Tansy accompanied his brothers on a ride to Snettering-on-Snoakes, and Parsley watched them in her spyglass.

They were young men now. Parsley admired how tall and straight Tansy sat in his saddle. Randolph and Rudolph looked squat and awkward by comparison.

As the horses ambled along, Randolph and Rudolph argued over what color the Royal Steed should be.

"The Royal Steed must be brown," Randolph declared. "And anyone who doesn't agree is a ninny."

"Wrong!" Rudolph yelled. "The Royal Steed must be black, and you're a ninny nincompoop."

"I think," Tansy said, "that—"

"Tell him, Tansy," Randolph said. "You know I'm right."

"Tell him I'm right," Rudolph said.

"I think the Royal Steed must be taller than—"

In her spyglass Parsley saw Randolph and Rudolph turn on Tansy.

They both shouted, "You're a nitwit ninny nincompoop, and you'll never ride the Royal Steed."

I'm not a nitwit, Tansy thought. The Royal Steed can be any color, but it has to be tall, so subjects can find their sovereign. And rattles have to be tied to its knees, which will also help people locate the king. Why don't Randolph and Rudolph ever think about their subjects?

The three princes rode on in silence.

Parsley kept watching them. Turn! she thought. Come closer. Come this way. Please come.

They turned onto Rosella Lane. Parsley rushed downstairs to the library, where she threw open a window and leaned out.

She could see them, actually see them, without the spyglass! They were walking their horses down the lane. Tansy looked even nicer than he did in the spyglass, and his freckles didn't stand out quite so much. She smiled a warm, friendly smile.

Randolph and Rudolph didn't notice Parsley, but Tansy did. She seemed to be smiling at him. It was such a kind smile too, a beautiful smile, even if her teeth were as green as grass. Tansy didn't remember anyone smiling at him like that ever before.

The princes reined in their horses only a few yards from Parsley.

"The fairy Bombina lives here," Randolph announced. "A king must invite nearby fairies to a banquet every year."

"Every other year," Rudolph said. "That's quite enough."

Tansy smiled back at Parsley.

She liked his smile. Hers broadened into the loveliest, most rapturous smile ever.

Bombina came into the library carrying a bouquet of peonies from the garden. She saw Parsley's smile and became wildly jealous. Who was getting that smile? She ran to the window.

Noblemen!

Not for long. Toads!

Parsley heard Bombina and turned, a frown replacing her smile.

If Parsley had smiled at Bombina—if she hadn't frowned—

But she did frown.

Bombina decided to do the one who wasn't a twin first. She shifted her weight to her left foot, stared hard at him, and lowered her chin, still staring.

Oh no! Parsley thought. "Don't!" She leaped in front of the fairy.

Bombina found herself staring straight at Parsley.

Aaaa! Bombina tried to stop casting the spell, but it was too late.

Six

What?!! Parsley felt trapped by Bombina's gaze. She tried to squirm away from it, but she couldn't. Wind rushed by her ears, and Bombina's eyes grew bigger and bigger.

Parsley's skin pinched. Something was squeezing her harder and harder, squeezing her insides and outsides, her face and her feet and her bones and her stomach. Her ears rang and boomed.

Then it was over. Whew! She wondered if she'd looked funny while it was going on, wondered if Tansy had noticed. She turned to see.

Where was he?

Where was she?

She faced a wall that hadn't been there a second ago. It looked familiar, though. She recognized the wallpaper lily pads, but they were much too big.

Then she knew. She looked down at herself. She was chartreuse! She was a Biddlebum Toad!

She looked way way up and saw Bombina's horrified face.

See what your transformations got you, Parsley thought angrily. She wanted to scream and wail. But she didn't make a sound. She didn't know what she'd do if a croak came out of her.

Oh no! Bombina thought, feeling dizzy. Parsley will never smile at me again.

Bombina saw the three princes gawking at her, so she pulled the window shut. Then she drew the drapes, being careful not to step on poor Parsley.

Her darling was so tiny and ugly. Bombina couldn't stand to look at her. Sadly, even tragically, the fairy hiccuped twice.

Parsley vanished.

In Rosella Lane Tansy shook his head to clear it. Where had the smiling maiden gone? What had the fairy done with her?

Bombina flew to the fairy queen's palace and begged an audience with her. As soon as she saw Anura, she began to weep, although she'd never wept in all her three thousand seven hundred and fourteen years. Between sobs she blurted out the whole tale.

"Please do something. You can punish me. You can lock me up. Only let me see Parsley's human smile once more." She wiped her tears. "Toads don't have lips or teeth. Did I ever tell you what beautiful green teeth my Parsley had?"

"My poor Bombina," Anura said. "You have reaped the bitter rewards of your folly."

Bombina nodded, tears streaming.

"It would give me the greatest pleasure to help you. But you know that the only way dear Bayleaf can—"

"Her name is Parsley," Bombina wailed.

"Yes, of course. But there is only one way your Paprika—"

"Parsley!"

"Sorry! But there is just one way your little, er, maiden can resume her human shape. And that is if some other human proposes marriage to her."

Bombina smiled through her tears. How could she have forgotten? All she had to do—

"No, my poor wretched Bombina. You cannot force a young man to propose, and the little toad cannot reveal what happened to her and what the remedy is. The proposal must be of the man's free will, or it will not transform anything."

⚓ ⚓ ⚓

Parsley discovered that toads could cry. Or once-human toads could, anyway.

Oh, why had Bombina broken her promise?

She wept for a full hour. Then she looked around. She was on the bank of a wide stream. A few yards away a rotting bridge crossed the water. Ferns and a weeping willow grew along the stream bank. Beyond them was a field of tall grasses. If Parsley had been at her human height, she would have seen goats grazing in the distance.

Parsley wondered what she'd eat here. There was no parsley.

Her tongue whipped out and caught a fly. She blinked and swallowed.

Ugh! she thought. I ate an insect! It tasted sweet. She started crying again. I won't do that twice. I'll starve first.

Her tongue snaked out and snagged a mosquito. She blinked and swallowed.

The mosquito was salty. Parsley stopped crying. Maybe she had been wrong to limit herself to parsley for all those years. She wondered how an ant would taste.

Seven

When the twins and Tansy returned to Biddle Castle from Snettering-on-Snoakes, King Humphrey IV sent for them. He rose from his throne and hugged Randolph. Or maybe it was Rudolph. He could never tell them apart. He knew about the difference in the size of their nostrils, but he could never remember which big nostril belonged to which twin.

He didn't hug Tansy.

"Lads!" He beamed at the twins and frowned at Tansy, hoping the boy wouldn't break anything just by standing still. "We were thinking about which of you should be our heir."

Randolph and Rudolph glared at each other. Tansy's heart started to pound.

"We have two stalwart sons to choose between."

Tansy's heart stopped pounding.

"So we have contrived a contest. The son who fetches us one hundred yards of linen fine enough to go through our Royal Ring"—King Humphrey IV took a ring off his pinky—"will wear this medallion." He reached into the pocket of his new Royal Ceremonial Robe and pulled out a golden medallion on which was inscribed *His Highness's Heir*. This was the cleverest part of the plan. Soon he'd know which twin was which. "The winner will rule when we are gone, and all Biddle will do his bidding."

Tansy's heart started to pound again. The contest meant trouble! Rudolph wouldn't stand for it if Randolph won, and Randolph wouldn't stand for it if Rudolph won. Whoever won, there would be trouble in Biddle.

"Father?"

King Humphrey IV scowled at Tansy. "Yes?"

"Can I seek the linen too?"

King Humphrey IV considered how peaceful home would be if Tansy were away. "You may." But he'd never let the lad rule Biddle, not even if Tansy's linen could pass through a ream of pinky rings.

⚓ ⚓ ⚓

Parsley spent an enjoyable afternoon sampling insects. Fleas were spicy. Ticks were sour. Midges tickled pleasantly as they went down, and caterpillars happened to taste a lot like parsley.

Late in the day a goatherd drove her goats across the stream. Parsley hid under the bridge, terrified of being trampled.

When the goats had all crossed, the goatherd sat on the far bank and dangled her feet in the stream.

Was I ever that big? Parsley wondered. She hopped backward, feeling nervous. She could be squashed so easily.

The goatherd saw the movement. She waded across the stream and groped through the ferns under the bridge. "A toad!" She picked Parsley up and placed her on her enormous palm. "Perhaps more than a toad. Kind sir, speak to me!" She waited. "Perhaps you can't talk. But you can hear my sad tale. I am not truly a goatherd." She sighed, and the wind from the sigh almost knocked Parsley off her perch. "I have been transformed."

You too? Parsley thought. Were you once a toad?

"In my true form I am a princess,

"I AM NOT TRULY A GOATHERD."

Princess Alyssatissaprincissa."

To Parsley's horror Princess Alyssatissaprincissa brought her huge face right up to Parsley. Parsley's right eye looked at a pimple as big as a bumblebee. Then Princess Alyssatissaprincissa kissed Parsley's side. The suction of the kiss pulled her skin away from her ribs.

After the kiss Princess Alyssatissaprincissa waited a moment and then dropped Parsley. She slogged back across the stream, muttering about the scarcity of frog princes.

The ferns cushioned Parsley's fall. She lay still, catching her breath.

⚓ ⚓ ⚓

Bombina spent the day knocking her knees together to enhance her vision and her hearing. She finally saw Parsley crouching under a fern and looking like any other chartreuse Biddlebum Toad, except for a faint sparkle that only a fairy could detect.

It was too sad to bear. Bombina had to look away. I'll never be jealous again and I'll never turn anything into a toad again, she thought, not even so much as a needle or a beetle. That will be my punishment.

⚓ ⚓ ⚓

Early the next morning King Humphrey IV saw his sons off. "Return in a week," he said.

Randolph and Rudolph each climbed into his own Royal Carriage. Tansy mounted his mare, Bhogs, whose name stood for Brown Horse of Good Speed.

When they reached Snettering-on-Snoakes, the villagers lined the road to see them off, and Bombina watched from her palace. She recognized the princes and itched to turn them into toads. If it hadn't been for them, Parsley would still be human. But she kept her promise and let them go by.

A mile beyond the village the road forked. The Royal Road continued to the left and wound through the principal towns of Biddle on its way to Kulornia. The right fork was Biddle Byway, which meandered through tiny villages and hamlets and never arrived anywhere.

Randolph and Rudolph took the left fork. Tansy started to follow them. But then he pulled Bhogs up short and turned her onto Biddle Byway.

If I stick with them, he thought, and we find the perfect length of linen, who'll get it? No—who won't get it? Me.

Eight

By the end of her first day as a toad, Parsley had eaten seven fleas, twelve ticks, two spiders, a worm, a caterpillar, four gnats, and eleven midges. Then she'd gone to sleep. When she woke up late the next morning, she was surprised all over again that she was a toad. She stayed still and thought about the advantages and disadvantages of her new state.

On the plus side was diet. Bugs were scrumptious! But that was about it for the plus side.

On the minus side was the goatherd Princess Alyssatissa whatever the rest of her name was. Also on the minus side were the loss of her spyglass and the loss of Tansy in her spyglass.

And she missed Bombina. She remembered Bombina's magic tricks and how exciting it had been, especially when she was little, to live with a fairy. She remembered being disappointed when Bombina had said that only magical creatures could make magic.

Parsley's pulse quickened. She was a magical creature now.

What could she try?

Bombina began all her spells by standing on her left foot, so Parsley tried to do the same. But balancing on one foot was hard. Her shape was all wrong for it. She struggled for twenty minutes before she finally managed it and stood, wobbling a little for ten whole seconds. Then she started to go over, and she had

to hop three times, while her head nodded and wagged, before she got steady
again.

A silver lady's comb appeared in the
air before her and fell into the moss
at her feet.

She'd done it! Accidentally, but she'd
done it. Too bad she had no hair.

She started to topple again. She
frowned and hopped back two steps,
stumbled, and got back onto her left
foot.

A crock of brown boot polish landed
next to the comb.

Parsley meant to laugh, but it came
out as a croak, her first croak. It was a
warm and melodious sound. She liked
it and croaked again. She extended her
four legs and stood tall and croaked
again. The pitch was a trifle lower that
way. She sat back to try to raise the

pitch, but before she could open her mouth again, she found herself rising into the air, eighteen inches at least. She flew across the stream and crash-landed on the opposite bank.

She lay still. Gadzooks! Making magic was fun!

⚓ ⚓ ⚓

On the first morning of the contest, Tansy passed through the hamlets of Harglepool, Flambow-under-Gree, Lower Vudwich, and Craugh-over-Pughtughlouch. In the afternoon he passed through Snug Podcoomb, Woolly Podcoomb, Podcoomb-upon-Hare, Upper Squeak, Lower Squeak, Popping Squeak, and Swinn-out-of-Crubble.

Wherever he went, Tansy asked Biddlers how they thought Biddle

" . . . AND CRASH-LANDED ON THE OPPOSITE BANK."

should be ruled, and he looked at linen. Each hamlet had its own master weaver, but not one of them could weave linen fine enough to squeeze through a bracelet, let alone a ring. Tansy worried that he would have found better cloth if he'd taken the Royal Road with his brothers.

Meanwhile, Randolph and Rudolph passed through towns with important-sounding short names like Ooth, Looth, Quibly, Eels, Hork, and Moowich. In Ooth the twins stopped at the first master weaver's shop they saw. The weaver pulled down his finest bolts of linen to show them.

"Hmm," Randolph said, "that one might do." He picked up a corner of cloth.

"Yes, it might." Rudolph picked up the other corner and glared at his brother.

"I saw it first." Randolph pulled the linen away from Rudolph.

"No, you didn't." Rudolph grabbed his corner again and yanked.

The linen tore down the middle.

"What have you done?" the weaver yelled. He wouldn't let the twins leave his store until one of them bought the ruined fabric, even though it didn't come close to fitting through a pinky ring. Randolph wound up paying, since he had touched the cloth first. His footman loaded it into his carriage.

There were fourteen master weavers in Ooth, and by the time the twins' carriages rolled out of town, seven bolts of torn linen were in each carriage. And not one square foot of cloth was fine enough to go through a pinky ring.

⚓ ⚓ ⚓

Parsley spent the afternoon learning to make magic. She made mistakes at first and created a big pile of objects that a toad didn't need, like a frying pan, a bow and arrows, and a bass fiddle.

But finally, she figured out how to make blue and pink and yellow balloons appear over the stream. They were a lovely sight, dozens of them, drifting over the water in friendly flocks.

By sundown she'd learned how to make almost anything she wanted, including a sprig of parsley, which had tasted awful. She'd taught herself how to make things vanish too. It was simple. All she had to do was hiccup twice, just as Bombina used to. She'd also perfected her flying, and even more important, she'd discovered how to land. She'd learned to knock her knees into her belly in order to see or hear anywhere in Biddle. She looked at Biddle Castle immediately, but she couldn't find Tansy or his horrible brothers there.

There was one bit of magic she couldn't perform, though. No matter what she tried, she couldn't turn herself back into a human.

Nine

Bombina peeked at Parsley while Parsley was making magic. She hadn't known that her toads could do that. Hah! she thought proudly. I bet Parsley is the only one smart enough to figure it out.

⚓ ⚓ ⚓

At dusk Princess Alyssatissaprincissa came by with her goats. "Oh, Sir Toad," she called, "Your Royal Highness, where are you?"

Uh-oh! Parsley decided to fly out of danger. She stood tall and croaked. But before she could finish the spell, Princess Alyssatissaprincissa picked her up.

"I apologize, Your Majesty. I didn't know the right way before. Now I'll turn you back into a prince in no time." She hurled Parsley into the side of the bridge.

Oof! Parsley landed in a patch of dirt. *Yow!* She wondered if her back was broken. She lay still and tried not to cry.

Princess Alyssatissaprincissa waded into the stream. Just a toad, she thought, just a stupid toad.

After Princess Alyssatissaprincissa had gone, Parsley sat up carefully. Her back wasn't broken, but she was sore all over. For the first time she understood why Bombina turned people into toads.

⚓ ⚓ ⚓

Days passed. Randolph and Rudolph fought over linen in twenty towns. They hired extra carriages to carry all the cloth they had to buy. But none of it would pass through a pinky ring.

Tansy had no better luck. In Woolly Podcoomb he bought the best bolt of linen he saw, hoping it was better than anything his brothers had found.

The sixth day of the contest dawned sunny and hot. Tansy purchased an apple in the hamlet of Whither Prockington and looked at linen. In Thither Prockington he looked at more linen. He was surprised, two miles farther along, to come upon Hither Prockington, which wasn't on any of the maps in the Royal Library. But Hither Prockington didn't have any fine linen either.

He rode on. After an hour he came to a stream.

Parsley saw the horse and rider coming and hopped under the bridge. Tansy let Bhogs drink and slipped off her back to stretch his legs.

"It's you!" Parsley cried—and discovered that she could speak.

Tansy thought he'd heard a voice, but he didn't see anyone.

Parsley hopped toward him. "Prince Tansy! Your Highness!" She wished she could hop faster. He was only a few yards away, but that was a fair distance now. She thought of flying, but she didn't want to startle him more than he was about to be startled.

Tansy was sure a maiden was calling him. Was she hiding under the bridge? He started toward it.

"Pray watch your feet."

He stood still.

"Look down, Your Highness."

A chartreuse Biddlebum Toad blinked up at him. A talking toad! Was he bewitched?

"I'm so glad to see you." Parsley tried to curtsy and almost toppled. "Especially

67

without your wicked brothers."

Tansy gasped and fell back a step.

"They're lying snitching stinkers."

It's the heat, Tansy thought. I'm hearing things. He rushed to the stream and dunked his head. The cold water felt good.

Parsley hopped down to the stream.

Tansy stood up. He felt his mind clear. He wouldn't hear any talking animals now.

"In truth, I hate your brothers."

The toad again! He *was* bewitched.

"In truth, I admire you. I admire you so."

There she was, chartreuse and warty and smiling at him. Such a nice smile. Something in his heart fluttered.

⚓ ⚓ ⚓

Bombina saw Tansy with Parsley. It was that prince again! She began to feel

"THERE SHE WAS, CHARTREUSE
AND WARTY AND SMILING AT HIM."

jealous, but she stopped herself. She had sworn not to, and she'd keep her oaths from now on.

Maybe the prince would be good for something. After all, her Parsley's smile was still the sweetest most adorable sight there was. Maybe . . .

⚓ ⚓ ⚓

Tansy sat on the riverbank and moaned. "I'm bewitched."

"No, you're not." Parsley opened her mouth to tell him about her transformation, but the words wouldn't come. She croaked to clear her throat and tried again, but she still couldn't. She stood on her left leg, spun around, and hopped twice, hoping to get some magic going, but nothing happened.

He watched her. He'd never seen a toad spin before.

She gave up. "You're not bewitched,

Your Highness. I'm a talking toad."
Maybe this would convince him. "If you
were bewitched, you'd hear your horse
speak too, wouldn't you?"

Perhaps she was right. He went to
Bhogs, who was grazing near the weeping willow. "Bhogs, speak to me. Am I
bewitched?"

Bhogs switched her tail and went on
grazing, which meant either she couldn't
speak or she didn't have anything to say.
Either way, he could still be bewitched.

"If you were bewitched, the fish would
be talking to you, and so would the
dragonflies and the caterpillars and
the"—Parsley's tongue snaked out.
She snagged a gnat and swallowed it—
"and the gnats and the . . ."

Maybe he was only a little bewitched,
just enough to understand Toad.

Parsley decided to change the subject.
"What brings you here, Prince Tansy?"

71

He didn't want to be rude and not answer, even if he was only imagining that the toad was speaking. If there really was a toad.

He sat again. "My father has set a contest for my brothers and me." He told her about the test and the prize. "The linen I bought isn't nearly good enough."

"I can help you!" Oh, it was wonderful to be a magical creature! "I can give you linen fine enough to go through the eye of a needle."

"If only you really could." He sighed.

Parsley felt irritated. How could she prove herself? She couldn't. He wouldn't believe the linen she made was real, no matter what. But maybe he'd believe it when his father gave him that golden medallion.

She had an idea. "Close your eyes, Your Highness."

Tansy closed his eyes, certain that when he opened them, he'd see a length of perfect linen. Perfect, but imaginary.

Parsley balanced on her left foot, feeling nervous. She had to get this just right. She tapped her nose with the fourth and last finger or toe of her right hand or front foot. Then she bent over and tapped her chin on the ground. Next she croaked at the highest pitch she could manage. And it worked.

"You can open your eyes."

Tansy did, and there, on the ground near his knee, was about three inches of coarse dirty linen.

Ten

Parsley tried not to laugh at Tansy's astonished face. "Put the linen in your saddlebag, Your Highness, and be sure it doesn't fall out."

"Thank you." Feeling silly, Tansy put the useless cloth on top of the bolt he'd purchased. "I must be going." He mounted Bhogs and galloped off without looking back.

"Farewell, dear Prince Tansy."

He shuddered and rode on. When he reached Biddle Castle, servants were unloading bolt after bolt of fabric from Randolph's and Rudolph's carriages. He took his saddlebag and followed the servants to the throne room.

King Humphrey IV was surrounded by a sea of cloth. He didn't know why the lads had carried so much home and why all of it was torn, and why none of it was nice enough to wipe his nose on.

"I have better linen somewhere, Father," Randolph said desperately. "I don't know where it's gotten to."

"I have better linen too," Rudolph said. "I don't know where mine has gotten to."

As soon as he saw the torn cloth, Tansy knew that his brothers had fought over every bolt. But most of it still looked better than the stuff he had.

King Humphrey IV said, "You lads are disappointing duffers."

"Father?" Tansy said. "I have linen too." He knelt before the throne and opened his saddlebag.

And the softest, creamiest linen he'd ever seen billowed out.

What? Tansy thought. Where's the scrap the toad gave me? Am I imagining this cloth? His fingers trembled as he drew it out.

"Let us see." Frowning, King Humphrey IV reached for the cloth. He didn't want Tansy to win, but the fabric was the finest he had ever touched. "Superb, son. Sublime."

There *had* been a toad! A magical talking toad.

"It will pass through the eye of a needle, Sire," Tansy said. He'd won! He was going to be king. King of Biddle!

"There's my cloth," Randolph said, "the cloth that I was searching for."

"There's *my* cloth," Rudolph said.

Together they said, "Tansy stole it."

☙ ☙ ☙

Parsley saw and heard it all, and she
hopped up and down in fury. But she
dared not fly to Tansy's aid. No one
would believe a toad, and Randolph or
Rudolph would step on her.

☙ ☙ ☙

"I didn't steal anything!" Tansy said.
"I wouldn't."

King Humphrey IV was confused.
Tansy probably had filched the fabric.
But from which brother? The king
looked back and forth from one twin
to the other until he was dizzy, but he
couldn't tell.

"We shall have another contest."
King Humphrey IV paced, threading
his way between the mountains of
material. Hmm . . . What should it be?

he wondered. Hmm . . .

He had it! His grandfather, King Humphrey III, had failed at this quest and had brought home that frightful flea instead.

"Whoever brings us a dog small enough to fit in a walnut shell shall win the throne." There.

Tansy kept protesting that he'd already won until King Humphrey IV said that if he didn't shut up, he wouldn't be allowed to take part in the new contest.

He did shut up, and he set out again with his brothers the next morning. Even though he was angry at his father and the twins, he was glad to be going back to the toad. He wanted to thank her and to apologize for not believing in her. And, of course, he wanted to ask for her help again, to beg for it, if he had to.

At the fork in the road outside Snettering-on-Snoakes, Randolph's carriage and Rudolph's carriage followed Bhogs onto the Biddle Byway.

They mustn't follow me! Tansy thought. One of them might step on the toad and squash her. Or they'd fight over the little dog and hurt it, or one of them would grab it and race home.

Tansy and the twins reached Harglepool. Tansy was trying to figure out how to slip away when he saw puppies playing outside a rickety shed. He made out the shapes of more puppies inside, and he saw a sign—*Best Barkers in Biddle. Ten pence per puppy.*

Some of the pups were tiny. Maybe Randolph and Rudolph could find their dogs here and stop following him.

He tied Bhogs up outside the shed. The carriages rumbled to a stop. Tansy began to go into the shed, but Randolph and then Rudolph pushed past him. He went in behind them.

A woman was sitting on a stool and combing a small dog in her lap.

Randolph said, "Harrumph—"

Rudolph said, "Harrumph, my fine woman—"

Randolph said, "Show me your smallest dog."

Rudolph said, "Show *me* your smallest dog." He glared at Randolph and stamped his foot. The whole shed shook.

Randolph glared at Rudolph.

Tansy tiptoed out of the shed.

Eleven

Tansy galloped along the Biddle Byway and finally reached Parsley's stream. He tied Bhogs to the willow and walked slowly and carefully toward the bridge. "Oh, Mistress Toad," he called.

When he came close, Parsley said, "Here I am, Your Highness."

Tansy knelt down. "I apologize for not believing in you. Thank you for helping me, Mistress Toad."

"My name is Parsley, Highness. You're welcome, but I didn't help as much as I'd hoped. You've been most unfairly treated."

"You know!"

"Certainly. You won the contest, and you have to win the next one too. For Biddle's sake." She beamed up at him. "You'd be our best king ever."

That ravishing smile! His heart fluttered again. He blushed and mumbled, "I'd try to be, Parsley."

"You *would* be. If you finally win—"

"I don't think I'll win, unless you help me again. I need—"

"A dog small enough to fit in a walnut." Parsley nodded. "I'll be happy to help."

She had him close his eyes while she made the most charming teensy-weensy dog—curly brown fur with a black patch on its back. Then she hid it.

"Open your eyes."

Tansy saw a coconut in the tall grass.

"Crack it carefully when you get home. The dog's name is Tefaw, which stands for Tiny Enough for a Walnut."

Tansy placed the coconut in his saddle-bag and thanked Parsley at least a dozen times.

She was embarrassed and changed the subject. "If you won and became king, what would you do?"

Tansy sat down. She squatted next to his right hand and never took her eyes off his face.

"I would build small Royal Glass Hills all over Biddle for children to slide down. I'd breed thousands of fireflies and release them for light on dark nights. And every year I'd give a Best Biddler Award in three categories: interesting dreams, knowledge of Biddle history, and acrobatics."

Parsley loved Tansy's plans, and she had some ideas of her own, like letting subjects go on quests and putting their discoveries in the Royal Museum of Quest Souvenirs, or like having the

Royal Army build chicken coops for people's chickens during peacetime.

Parsley and Tansy talked for hours. When the goatherd Princess Alyssatissa-princissa came by, Parsley made a big haystack and hid herself and Tansy inside it.

⚓ ⚓ ⚓

Bombina watched them talk. Keep smiling, Parsley, she thought. Smile, my love.

⚓ ⚓ ⚓

Tansy liked Parsley's smile more and more, until he believed that toads were the most beautiful creatures in Biddle. And the smartest and the friendliest.

For her part Parsley admired Tansy more and more. And when he said he'd make toads the Royal Animal and make people pay a fine for squashing them, her heart almost burst with love.

Night came. Tansy stretched out under the bridge, and Parsley settled down a yard or two away, in case he rolled over in his sleep.

They talked the whole next day and the day after that and the day after that, for six days, until Tansy had to return to Biddle Castle.

While he saddled Bhogs, he tried to say how much it had meant to him to talk to her, but he couldn't find the words. He mounted Bhogs and looked down at Parsley. "Thank you, and farewell." He rode off, turning to wave until he could no longer distinguish her from the grass.

Twelve

Tansy heard barking as soon as he crossed the Royal Drawbridge. In the throne room puppies were chewing on the Royal Drapes, making messes on the Royal Rug, leaping at Royal Chair Legs and Royal Table Legs and the Royal Legs of Randolph and Rudolph. King Humphrey IV was standing on his throne, lifting his new Royal Ceremonial Robe out of reach.

None of the puppies was small enough to fit in a walnut shell.

"I had a smaller dog somewhere, Father," Randolph said.

"I had a smaller dog too," Rudolph said.

"Remove these puppies," King Humphrey IV roared.

Royal Servants shooed the dogs from the room. King Humphrey IV descended and sat on his throne.

Tansy knelt down. "I have a dog too." He took out the coconut. Using his hunting knife, he cracked it carefully and found a walnut shell inside. He began to smile as he cracked the walnut shell—and found a peanut shell. That Parsley! Grinning broadly, he cracked the peanut shell and found a pistachio shell, and inside the pistachio shell was Tefaw. The dog pranced around on Tansy's hand and barked an astonishingly deep bark for such a tiny creature.

"There it is," Randolph said. "There's my dog."

"There's *my* dog," Rudolph said.

Together they said, "Tansy stole it."

"I HAVE A DOG TOO."

"I did not steal it!" Tansy yelled. "I got it my—"

"Did too steal it," Randolph hollered.

"Did too steal it," Rudolph screamed.

King Humphrey IV was puzzled. The twins had never lied before. But Tansy did look truthful, and they hadn't said a word about a coconut.

There was only one thing to do. "We will have a final contest. The son who brings home the most beautiful bride will be our heir." The twins would hardly be able to say they'd misplaced a maiden.

⚓ ⚓ ⚓

Parsley was angrier than she'd ever been before. Tansy won, she thought, fuming. Fair and square.

⚓ ⚓ ⚓

Bombina wondered why Parlsey looked so angry. The fairy watched and waited.

⚓ ⚓ ⚓

Randolph and Rudolph didn't try to follow Tansy this time. Their carriages turned onto the Royal Road and sped on.

Tansy kicked Bhogs into a gallop. He didn't know what to do. He didn't want to pick a bride just because she was pretty.

Bhogs streaked through Harglepool.

The kindest queen in Biddle history was Queen Lorelei, and her nose had been a bit too big. And although Queen Sonora had been beautiful, she was remembered for her wisdom.

Bhogs dashed through Lower Vudwich.

Besides, no matter how pretty his choice was, his father would probably say Randolph's or Rudolph's choice was prettier.

Bhogs flew though Podcoomb-upon-Hare.

And what if he won and had to marry a maiden he didn't like?

Bhogs tore through Popping Squeak.

He didn't know what to do. The only thing he knew was that he wanted to discuss it with Parsley.

If only he could find a maiden as smart as she was—as smart and sweet and understanding, with a smile that was even half as heartwarming.

There was her stream. He slid off Bhogs's back. "Parsley, where are you?"

She was so happy to see him. She put all her happiness into her smile.

As soon as Tansy saw the smile, he knew. He couldn't marry anyone but Parsley, even if she was a toad. He had to marry his love, if she'd have him.

He dropped to his knees. "Parsley, will you marry me?"

⚓ ⚓ ⚓

Bombina whooped and yelled, "He did
it! My precious Parsley! I love that
prince!"

⚓ ⚓ ⚓

For a moment Parsley just blinked up
at Tansy. Her smile froze. Wind rushed
by her ears. She'd felt this wind before.
What???

Oh no oh no. Her skin was expanding.
She was pulsing all over, her insides, her
head. *Boom! Boom!* It hurt! And her
blood was rushing, swooshing, flooding.

Tansy's dear face, coming closer, looking frightened. And now she was above
his head, rising higher. Oh oh oh!

It was over. •

Parsley panted, her hand pressed to her
chest.

Her hand! She had a hand?

She looked down at herself. She was human again!

It's the maiden from the fairy's palace, Tansy thought, the one with green teeth.

Tansy saved me! Parsley thought. She smiled down at him. "Of course I'll marry you, if you still want me."

"I do!" He could see his beloved toad in her smile and in her eyes.

She said, "Do you like parsley?"

Thirteen

Randolph and Rudolph each decided that it didn't matter who they thought was the most beautiful maiden. It only mattered what their father thought.

On the outskirts of Ooth Randolph saw a pretty maiden picking roses in her garden. He stopped his carriage and got out.

Rudolph got out of his carriage.

"I say," Randolph said, "will you marry me if my father the king chooses me to be his heir and chooses you as the most beautiful bride?"

Rudolph said, "Will you marry *me* if

the king chooses me to be his heir and chooses you as the most beautiful bride?"

"I asked her first," Randolph yelled.

"I asked her second," Rudolph shouted.

The maiden giggled. She pointed to each of them in turn and said,

> *"Which son?*
> *Either one.*
> *Pink, gold, blue.*
> *I choose you!"*

She pointed at Randolph.

He smirked at Rudolph and climbed back into his carriage. The maiden climbed in after him. The carriages rolled on.

Whenever Randolph and Rudolph passed a pretty maiden, they stopped their carriages and each asked her to marry him if King Humphrey IV chose him as heir and chose her as most beautiful.

Some maidens picked Randolph. Some picked Rudolph. Some refused them both and said,

> *"Which son?*
> *Neither one.*
> *Pink, gold, gray.*
> *I say nay!"*

By the time they reached Moowich, each twin had ten carriages full of maidens.

⚓ ⚓ ⚓

Tansy and Parsley and Bhogs ambled down the Biddle Byway. At the end of the week they reached Biddle Castle. As soon as she saw it, Parsley felt nervous.

She wanted to win the throne for Tansy, but she didn't think she was pretty enough.

In the throne room Randolph's maidens were milling about on the right side of the room, and Rudolph's were milling about on the left. There were scores of them. King Humphrey IV was glad to see so many winsome wenches, but what kind of kings would the twins be if they couldn't make up their minds about which maiden to marry?

Tansy entered holding Parsley's hand. He led her to the throne, and they both knelt down.

"Father, this is Parsley, the most beautiful maiden in Biddle, the maiden I wish to marry."

"Let us look at you, lass."

Parsley blushed and smiled at King Humphrey IV.

"She's hideous!" Randolph screamed. "Look at her teeth."

"Look at her teeth!" Rudolph shrieked. "She's horrendous!"

No one saw Bombina materialize behind Rudolph's maidens. Luckily for the twins, she didn't hear what they'd just said.

King Humphrey IV noticed the color of the damsel's teeth, but he paid more attention to the loveliness of her smile. With such a smile her teeth could be sprouting fur and he wouldn't mind.

"Sire!" Randolph hissed. "Think of your ripped Royal Robe."

"Sire!" Rudolph hissed. "Think of your broken scepter."

King Humphrey IV frowned. He looked over at Randolph's lasses and beckoned to one of them. He beckoned to a beauty of Rudolph's too. They approached, and each of them was at least as pretty as Parsley.

"Oh no you don't!" Bombina belowed. She marched to the throne. She wouldn't turn the king into a toad, but she'd turn him into something.

A fairy! King Humphrey IV trembled. He stood and bowed. Randolph and Rudolph trembled. They bowed too.

Tansy gasped. She was the one who'd turned Parsley into a toad! Well, she wasn't going to do it again. He drew his sword.

Parsley ran into Bombina's arms. "I missed you!" She smiled up at the fairy.

Tansy sheathed his sword.

Bombina felt dizzy. Her Parsley was smiling at her again. She began to weep happy tears. "Oh my dear!"

King Humphrey IV thought, The damsel is dear to a fairy? A fairy's friend would make a fine future queen. He cleared his throat. "Tansy shall be our heir."

Tansy could hardly believe it. He was going to be king, and he was going to marry his love. He felt overjoyed, overjoyed in a solemn way. He'd be a fair and kind king, and he'd make sure his subjects always had enough bathwater and mittens and—

Randolph screeched, "But I have to be king!"

Rudolph screeched, "But I have to be king!"

Randolph yelled, "Tansy broke the scepter and he tore—"

Parsley said, "He did not! You both did it and blamed him."

"They did?" King Humphrey IV looked at the twins. Could this be true? The fairy would know. "Did they?"

Tansy held his breath.

Bombina stared at each twin in turn and used her fairy powers to find out. She nodded. "They did." She felt a thrill. Randolph and Rudolph would make superb toads. She stared at Randolph.

"No!" Parsley yelled.

Bombina stopped staring. "No?"

Parsley considered. Randolph and Rudolph deserved to be toads if anyone did. But Princess Alyssatissaprincissa might propose to one of them, and then he would be a prince all over again. She had an idea. She whispered it to Bombina, who nodded.

The fairy flapped her wings twice, and howled *weejoon zowowow ay yay ay.*

Epilogue

Randolph and Rudolph spun around faster and faster, so fast that they created a tornado in the throne room, and all the pretty maidens wept and whimpered.

At last the twins stopped spinning, and two goatherds stood glaring at each other. Bombina hiccuped twice, and they vanished, one appearing in a meadow just north of Princess Alyssatissaprincissa and the other appearing in a meadow just east of Princess Alyssatissaprincissa.

Parsley and Tansy were married the

next day. King Humphrey IV conducted the ceremony, and Bombina gave away the bride. Zeke and Nelly were there, along with Parsley's younger brother, Pepper.

Eventually Randolph married Princess Alyssatissaprincissa, and Rudolph married the princess's sister, Countess Marianabanessacontessa, who was also a goatherd. Having their own separate herds of goats pleased the twins, and they came to like each other.

Bombina never turned anyone into a toad again, but she performed thousands of other magic tricks for Tansy and Parsley's children, who all inherited their mother's captivating smile.

Tansy was a wonderful king. He put his subjects first, and he rode a tall horse so they were always able to to find him. His subjects loved having their own souvenirs in the Royal Museum of Quest Souvenirs, and his subjects' chickens loved the coops the Royal Army built for them.

Bombina's cook taught Parsley's favorite parsley recipes to the Royal Cook, and the Royal Cook invented a few of her own. Parsley's smile grew greener and greener, and she never ate another insect.

And they all, monarchs and subjects and goatherds and fairies, lived happily ever after.